SUPERSTARS OF SPORTS

CONNOR
McDAVID
HOCKEY SUPERSTAR
BY BRENDA HAUGEN

CAPSTONE PRESS
a capstone imprint

Blazers Books are published by Capstone Press,
1710 Roe Crest Drive, North Mankato, Minnesota 56003
www.mycapstone.com

Library of Congress Cataloging-in-Publication Data
Names: Haugen, Brenda author.
Title: Connor McDavid : hockey superstar / by Brenda Haugen.
Description: North Mankato, Minnesota : An imprint of Capstone Press, [2019]
  | Series: Blazers. Superstars of sports | Includes index. | Audience:
  Ages: 9-14.
Identifiers: LCCN 2018003088 (print) | LCCN 2018020819 (ebook) | ISBN
  9781543525137 (eBook PDF) | ISBN 9781543525052 (hardcover) | ISBN
  9781543525090 (paperback)
Subjects: LCSH: McDavid, Connor, 1997—Juvenile literature. | Hockey
  players—Canada—Biography—Juvenile literature.
Classification: LCC GV848.5 (ebook) | LCC GV848.5 .H39 2019 (print) | DDC
  796.962092 [B]—dc23
LC record available at https://lccn.loc.gov/2018003088

Editorial Credits
Carrie Braulick Sheely, editor; Kyle Grenz, designer; Eric Gohl, media researcher;
Tori Abraham, production specialist

Quote Sources
Page 6, "Connor McDavid was born to play hockey." 17 March 2012. Toronto Star. https://www.thestar.com/sports/hockey/2012/03/17/connor_mcdavid_was_born_to_play_hockey.html
Page 17, "Connor McDavid named Most Sportsmanlike." 11 April 2014. Ontario Hockey League. http://ontariohockeyleague.com/connor-mcdavid-named-most-sportsmanlike/
Page 21, "Connor McDavid goes No. 1 to Oilers; Sabres get Jack Eichel at No. 2." ESPN. 26 June 2015. http://www.espn.com/nhl/story/_/id/13155772/2015-nhl-draft-edmonton-oilers-draft-connor-mcdavid-no-1-overall
Page 23, "Why Does Connor McDavid, the NHL's Brightest Young Star, Still Go Unrecognized in the U.S.? New York Daily News. 10 November 2017. http://www.nydailynews.com/sports/hockey/nhl-star-connor-mcdavid-unrecognized-u-s-article-1.3623713?src=rss

This book is dedicated to Marv Leier, who always has my back. You are a true blessing to me.—BLH

Printed and bound in the United States of America.
PA017

TABLE OF CONTENTS

CHAPTER 1

A STAR IN THE MAKING

On November 19, 2016, the Edmonton Oilers faced the Dallas Stars. The puck bounced toward Oilers' **center**, Connor McDavid. He shot it at the net. Score! Connor had earned his first **hat trick** in the National Hockey League (NHL).

center—the hockey player who participates in a face-off at the beginning of play

hat trick—when a player scores three goals in one game

Connor McDavid shoots for a goal against the Dallas Stars on November 19, 2016.

Connor McDavid (second from right) with his family

"You could tell right from the start that he was a little bit different. . . . He seemed to have an **affinity** for it [hockey]."

—Brian McDavid

6

Connor was born January 13, 1997, to Brian and Kelly McDavid. He lived with his parents and his brother in Newmarket, Ontario, Canada. Connor started skating at age 3. He started playing hockey the next year.

affinity—a talent for and liking for something

Connor didn't play like the other kids. They gathered around the puck. Connor waited until the puck popped out of the crowd. Then he took control of it and sped away. No one could keep up with him.

Connor McDavid became known for his speed as he continued to play hockey. Today he is one of the NHL's fastest skaters.

When Connor was 7 years old, he played with the York Simcoe Express team. Brian coached the team. Connor helped York Simcoe win four Ontario Minor Hockey Association titles in a row.

FACT

As a child, Connor's favorite team was the Toronto Maple Leafs. Bryan McCabe (left) and Mats Sundin (right) were two of the team's star players in the mid-2000s.

When he was 14, Connor played for the Toronto Marlboros junior team. He became the team's star center. In his first season, Connor scored 33 goals and made 39 **assists** in just 33 games.

assist—a pass that leads to a score by a teammate

Connor McDavid wears number 97 for the year he was born.

CHAPTER 2

JOINING THE ONTARIO HOCKEY LEAGUE

In 2013 Connor had a choice to make. He could wait to play on a college team or join the Ontario Hockey League (OHL). The OHL is one of Canada's top three junior leagues. Connor chose to play in the OHL.

At 15 years old, Connor needed special permission to play in the OHL. Usually, players must be 16. He was only the third player let into the league at this age.

Connor McDavid skates with the puck in an OHL game in 2014.

Connor McDavid makes a pass as the Otters play the Guelph Storm in a 2014 Western Conference Final game.

"Everyone involved in this game knows what a superstar this young man is, but Connor stays humble throughout."
—Sherry Bassin, Otters' general manager

Connor began playing for the OHL's Erie Otters. In his first season Connor racked up 66 **points** with 25 goals. He also won the William Hanley Trophy. The trophy is given to the OHL player who shows the best **sportsmanship**.

points—the total number of goals and assists a player has earned

sportsmanship—playing a sport or game respectfully and fairly

Connor McDavid stands with the Canadian Hockey League's Player of the Year trophy in 2015.

The 2014-15 season was special with the Otters too. Connor was named the team captain. He collected 44 goals and 120 points. He was named Player of the Year for the OHL and the Canadian Hockey League.

CHAPTER 3

WELCOME TO THE PROS

In 2015 the NHL Edmonton Oilers **drafted** Connor. The **rookie** went on to score 16 goals and added 32 assists. Five of his goals were game winners.

draft—to select a player to join a sports organization or team

rookie—a first-year player

FACT

Connor's 48 season points came in just 45 games. He missed nearly half the season after breaking his collarbone.

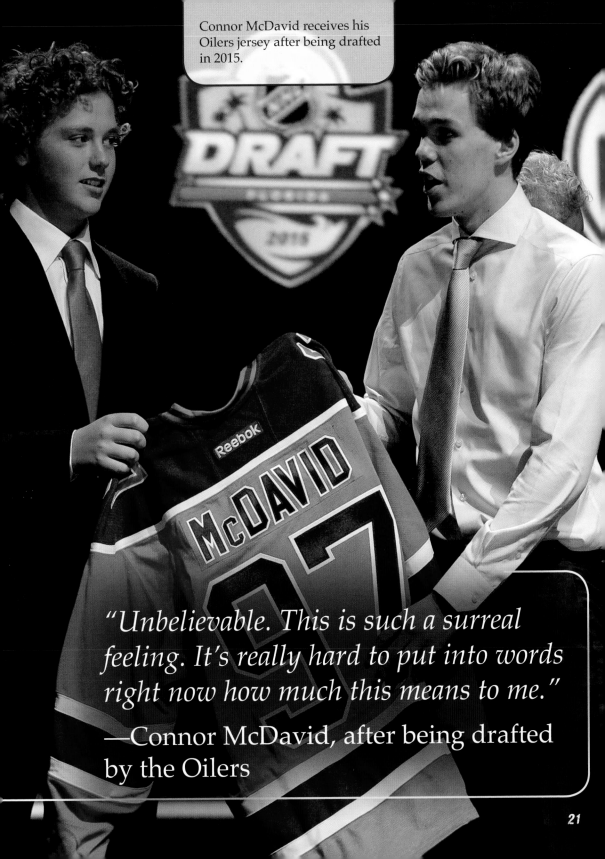

Connor McDavid receives his Oilers jersey after being drafted in 2015.

"Unbelievable. This is such a surreal feeling. It's really hard to put into words right now how much this means to me."

—Connor McDavid, after being drafted by the Oilers

Connor McDavid plays in a game against the Dallas Stars in November 2016.

"Obviously it's a big responsibility for a young guy like that to wear the 'C.' I think he does a tremendous job."

—Connor's teammate, Adam Larsson, on Connor becoming the team captain

Connor was named the Oilers' captain in 2016. At 19 years old, he was the youngest captain in NHL history. Connor started the season strong. After 11 games he had already earned 13 points.

Before the 2016-17 season, the Oilers had not made it to the playoffs since 2006.

Connor went on to win the Art Ross Trophy. It is given to the leading regular-season scorer. He had earned 100 points with 20 goals. Connor helped his team reach the Stanley Cup **playoffs**.

playoffs—a series of games played after the regular season to decide a championship

Connor McDavid looks to make a pass in a 2017 Stanley Cup playoff game against the Anaheim Ducks.

CHAPTER 4

A BRIGHT FUTURE

Connor won two more big awards at the end of the 2016-17 season. He earned the Hart Memorial Trophy as the most valuable player (MVP). He also won the Ted Lindsay Award as the NHL's best player.

Connor signed a $100 million **contract** in July 2017. He quickly proved he was worth the money. Connor scored a hat trick in the Oilers' first game of the 2017-18 season. Fans look forward to what the future holds for the young star.

contract—a legal agreement

Connor was the first player in Oilers history to score a hat trick in a season-opening game.

Connor McDavid celebrates with teammates after making a goal in a 2017 game.

TIMELINE

-1997-
Connor McDavid is born in Richmond Hill, Ontario, Canada.

-2001-
Connor begins playing hockey.

-2014-
Connor plays with Team Canada in the World Junior Ice Hockey Championships. The team earns fourth place.

-2012-
The Toronto Marlboros draft Connor.

GLOSSARY

affinity (uh-FIH-nuh-tee)—a talent for and liking toward something

assist (uh-SIST)—a pass that leads to a score by a teammate

center (SEN-tur)—the hockey player who participates in a face-off at the beginning of play

contract (KAHN-trakt)—a legal agreement

draft (DRAFT)—to select a player to join a sports organization or team

hat trick (HAT TRIK)—when a player scores three goals in one game

playoffs (PLAY-ohfs)—a series of games played after the regular season to decide a championship

points (POYNTZ)—the number of goals and assists added together

rookie (RUK-ee)—a first-year player

sportsmanship (SPORTS-muhn-ship)—playing a sport or game respectfully and fairly

Stanley Cup (STAN-lee KUP)—the trophy given each year to the NHL champion

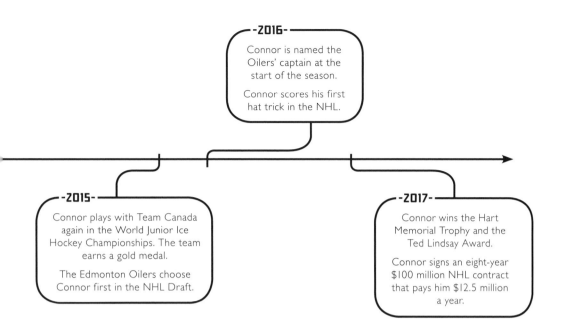

-2016-

Connor is named the Oilers' captain at the start of the season.

Connor scores his first hat trick in the NHL.

-2015-

Connor plays with Team Canada again in the World Junior Ice Hockey Championships. The team earns a gold medal.

The Edmonton Oilers choose Connor first in the NHL Draft.

-2017-

Connor wins the Hart Memorial Trophy and the Ted Lindsay Award.

Connor signs an eight-year $100 million NHL contract that pays him $12.5 million a year.

READ MORE

Mortillaro, Nicole. *Connor McDavid.* Hockey Superstars. North Mankato, Minn.: Capstone Press, 2016.

Nagelhout, Ryan. *Hockey: Who Does What?* Sports: What's Your Position?: New York: Gareth Stevens, 2018.

Omoth, Tyler. *Pro Hockey's Championship.* Major Sports Championships. North Mankato, Minn.: Capstone Press, 2018.

INTERNET SITES

Use FactHound to find Internet sites related to this book.

Visit *www.facthound.com*

Just type in **9781543525052** and go.

 Check out projects, games and lots more at
www.capstonekids.com

INDEX